First published in Great Britain 2003
by Egmont Books Limited
239 Kensington High Street, London W8 6SA
Story adapted from *Toby Had a Little Lamb*
Photographs © Gullane (Thomas) Ltd. 2002
All Rights Reserved

Thomas the Tank Engine & Friends

A BRITT ALLCROFT COMPANY PRODUCTION

Based on The Railway Series by The Rev W Awdry

© Gullane (Thomas) LLC 2003

ISBN 1 4052 0473 7
1 3 5 7 9 10 8 6 4 2
Printed in Italy

Toby had a Little Lamb

**Based on *The Railway Series*
by The Rev. W. Awdry**

EGMONT

It was winter on the Island of Sodor. The hills and fields were covered in snow. Toby and Henrietta were working hard on their branchline. They were very cold.

"This isn't much fun," said Toby. "I can't wait to get into my nice, dry shed."

But suddenly Toby's Driver applied the brakes! Farmer McColl was standing by the side of the line, waving a big red flag.

"Please help me!" said Farmer McColl. "My phone lines are down, all the roads are blocked, and my sheep have just started lambing! They're trapped on the hillside, cut off by the snow!"

"How can we help?" asked Toby,
at once.

"I need a vet as quickly as possible!"
said the worried farmer.

"We'll stop at the next signalbox,"
said Toby's Driver. "I'll phone the vet
from there."

Toby raced to
the signalbox. His
Driver called ahead
to Callan Station and
explained the problem.
When they arrived at the station,
The Fat Controller was already
waiting with the vet.
"I'll send Duck to the farm right away,"
said The Fat Controller. "This is a job
for an engine with a snowplough."

Duck battled bravely along the track.
But too much snow had fallen, and the
line ahead was blocked.
"We can't carry on," said
Duck's Driver, grimly.
"We'll have to go back."
Toby was very surprised
to see Duck return to the station.
"I tried my hardest," puffed Duck,
"but even my snowplough can't
get through."

The Fat Controller was very worried.

Then Toby had an idea.

"We could use my old branchline, sir!
I know that line like the back of my
buffers. It's our only chance to help
the baby lambs!"

The Fat Controller agreed and the
vet climbed aboard Henrietta.

Toby struggled along the old
branchline. The blizzard was very
bad and Toby's Driver was worried.
"Perhaps we should go back," said
his Driver.
"I can do it!" called Toby. "As long
as these lines hold!"

But Toby had forgotten about the rickety old bridge. As he started to cross it, he could feel his wheels wobbling. His Driver tried to keep him steady.

"I've got to reach the other side of this bridge!" gasped Toby. "Those lambs need me!"

At last Toby reached Farmer McColl.
He was waiting in the cold, and he
smiled when he saw Toby's headlamp
shining through the snowstorm.
"You made it!" he cried. "What a brave
engine you are!"

Farmer McColl took the vet to see the lambs. Toby waited for them to come back, hoping the lambs would be all right. At last he saw Farmer McColl in the distance.

"The baby lambs are safe and sound, Toby!" called Farmer McColl, "But we need a place to keep the little ones warm and dry."

Toby smiled. "Henrietta has plenty of
room," he said.

So Farmer McColl and
the vet brought the
little lambs to shelter
inside Henrietta.

Toby and Henrietta stayed at the farm
for several days, just to make sure the
lambs were all right. At last the blizzard
ended, and the sun shone down.

Farmer McColl was very grateful.
"Thank you, Toby," he said. "We
couldn't have done it without you!"
"No. Thank *you*!" said Toby. "There's
nothing I like better than helping out
a friend in need!"